# Terry Nation's.
# DALEK SPECIAL

# Terry Nation's
# DALEK
## Special

**Compiled and Edited by TERRANCE DICKS**

A TARGET BOOK
published by
the Paperback Division of
W. H. ALLEN & Co. Ltd.

A Target Book
Published in 1979
by the Paperback Division of W. H. Allen & Co. Ltd.
A Howard & Wyndham Company
44 Hill Street, London W1X 8LB

*Daleks: The Secret Invasion* copyright © 1979 by Lynsted Park
Enterprises Ltd.
DALEK SPECIAL text copyright © 1979 by Terrance Dicks.
Daleks created by Terry Nation
Cover and inside illustrations by Andrew Skilleter

Photographs featured on pages 44 and 45 copyright © Keystone
Press Agency
Photographs featured on pages 40/41, 54/55, 57, 61, 62/63, 67,
68/69, 70/71, 73, 74/75, 83, 86/87, 91 and 95 copyright © British
Broadcasting Corporation

Printed in Great Britain by
Richard Clay (The Chaucer Press) Ltd
Bungay
Suffolk
ISBN 0 426 20094 2

We should like to thank the Doctor Who Appreciation Society,
and in particular the society's historian, Jeremy Bentham,
for help in the preparation of this book.

# CONTENTS

# DALEKS

## THE SECRET INVASION
### (An original story)

## TERRY NATION

### Chapter One

The cousins had a marvellous time in
London celebrating Danny's birthday.
David and his sister, Emilie, had come up
from Kent. Danny and his brother, Paul,
had been at Victoria to meet them. They
had lunch in a Wimpy bar where Paul bet
he could eat enough Wimpys to get his
name in the Guinness Book of Records
and all the others said he couldn't, and
anyway they couldn't afford it.

After that they'd stood in a long queue to
see 'The Exorcist' only to be turned away
at the box office because they were too
young. Instead they went to see 'Robin
Hood' which was terrific. And now the
outing was nearly over and they were on
the platform at Green Park Underground
waiting for a train. They stood near a
silvery grey barricade of corrugated iron
sheets that hid some construction work.

The loudspeakers on the platform made
a nervous clicking noise that was followed
by a man's voice, eerie and echoing.
'Attention. All passengers must leave the
platforms immediately and proceed to the
street exits. This is an emergency.' Then
the voice started to say the same thing all
over again. The other people at the far
end of the platform hurried towards the
exits.

'What's that all about?' David asked.

'Bomb scare, I shouldn't be surprised,' said Danny.

His last words were drowned by the loudest explosion any of them had ever heard. A great shockwave of blast roared along the platform toward them. They briefly saw a billowing cloud of smoke and dust and heard the crunch of falling masonry. Then the lights flickered twice and vanished, plunging the place into darkness.

In the very moment of all this happening Danny had the good sense to yell, 'Down everybody . . . and hang on to one another!'

The four flung themselves down and grabbed at the arms and legs of the one nearest. They felt the hot blast rip across them like the breath of an angry dragon. Behind them the corrugated iron sheets were wrenched from their moorings with an enormous crash. Silence drove away the sounds, and after a moment Danny cautiously raised his head. He brushed the dust out of his hair.

'Everybody all right?' he asked. Three familiar, if slightly nervous, voices answered that they were.

'It's as black as pitch,' said David.

Paul said, 'I can't see a thing.'

Emilie said, 'Danny, I think it's time you opened the birthday present we gave you.'

'It's not exactly the moment for opening birthday presents,' Danny snapped.

'Yes, it is,' said Emilie. 'We've given you a flashlight.'

Danny snatched the package from his pocket and ripped the paper off. Moments later, he found the switch on the torch and a cold clear gleam of light shot from

his hand like an arrow.

They stood in shocked awe at what they saw. Ahead of them the platform was completely blocked by fallen debris. Danny spun around and pointed the beam in the other direction. The wall of corrugated iron had been blasted across the lines and platform. Twisted and tangled it made a jagged barricade. David walked up to the iron wall and kicked it. It gave a great booming sound but stayed firm. 'We're not getting out that way,' he said.

Danny directed his flashlight at the section of wall that had, until now, been hidden by the iron sheets. There was an opening. Danny led and the cousins picked their way through the timber props and tools that littered the narrow passage.

They had gone about forty yards when the tunnel suddenly ended. A concrete wall blocked the way. Danny danced his light around the area. There were cement bags piled everywhere, and behind one of the piles, Danny squeezed through to get a better look. It was a rusted iron door with a huge lever-like handle. Danny tugged at it. For a moment it wouldn't budge, and then as he applied all his strength it started to move. Finally there was a loud click.

'Got it!' said Danny triumphantly. The door started to swing slowly open making a low creaking noise.

'I don't like it,' said Paul. 'I've heard doors open like that in horror films and there's always something nasty behind them.' A wave of stale air wafted out at them.

'It must lead somewhere,' Danny said, and then realised he was whispering. 'Probably an old emergency exit,' he said more loudly, trying to give the others confidence. 'Come on.'

The four filed into the tunnel. Emilie's hand brushed against the green slime on the wall and she gave a little 'Ugghh' sound. They'd gone hardly any distance when they heard an echoing 'clang'. Danny pointed the torch behind them. The iron door had swung shut. He turned forward again. What the flashlight illuminated made him stop dead in his tracks. His mouth fell open. He tried to speak, but no words came. He sensed that his companions were in the same rigid state of fear that gripped him.

A harsh, grating, mechanical voice ahead of them commanded, 'Stand-where-you-are. Do-not-move.' The voice and the creature it belonged to were unmistakable. It was a

Dalek. And behind it . . . three more.

## Chapter Two

The cousins stood in frozen terror. The
Dalek glided closer. The single lens of its
'eye' scanned them carefully. Danny felt
the prickle of fear run up his spine. The
Dalek's arm telescoped out and pressed
against his chest, pushing him back against
the wall. The enormous strength of the
arm forced the air from his body. He
gasped and tried to wriggle free. The
pressure increased and Danny thought his
ribs would cave in. He did the only thing
he could think of and with one quick
movement he jabbed the flashlight hard
against the Dalek's eye. The powerful
beam momentarily blinded the creature. It
released its pressure on Danny and swung
its arm to knock the torch aside. In the
same instant Danny yelled to the others,
'Run!'

Emilie, Paul and David did not need
telling twice. All four of them turned and
ran as they had never run before.
Scrambling and stumbling they raced
toward the heavy iron door at the end of
the passage. The Dalek recovered from its
temporary blindness before they had
covered half the distance. Its stubby gun
barrel came up and fired. The tunnel was
lit by the blue-white glare of the neutronic
charge. There was the crackle of high

energy discharge and the cousins felt the muscle-numbing pain as the rays whipped past them at the speed of light. The iron door took the full impact of the blast. Its surface instantly glowed white with heat and rivulets of molten metal trickled down.

Desperately, Paul reached for the handle, then snatched his burned fingers away with a cry of pain. The neutron rays had welded the door immovably shut. There was no escape. The cousins turned to face the Dalek as it advanced slowly down the tunnel, its gun pointed unwaveringly toward them. When it fired there was hardly any sound and the light from it was no more than a gentle glow. The Dalek had fired at minimum power, but even so the four felt the rays jerk through their bodies like a violent electric shock. Their heads ached and their legs buckled under them as the dark blanket of unconsciousness wrapped around them. They slumped to the ground.

David started to waken. He felt the touch of soft damp grass against his cheek. He could hear the distant wail of sirens. He sat up quickly, and stared about him. Emilie was beside him, fully conscious but looking frightened and bewildered.

'Where are we?' David asked.

'Green Park, I think. Isn't that the station and Piccadilly up there?'

David stared. They were about two hundred yards away from the road where there seemed to be a tremendous amount of activity. Red and blue flashing lights. Fire engines and police cars and crowds of people milling around the area. A loudspeaker voice was ordering the sightseers to keep back.

'It must be something to do with the

explosion,' Emilie said. 'The emergency services.'

A sudden fear snatched at David's stomach. He scrambled to his feet. 'Where are Danny and Paul?'

Emilie shook her head and looked as though she were about to cry. 'The Daleks must still be holding them prisoners.'

'Then we must do something,' David said urgently. 'We've got to help them.' He grabbed Emilie's hand and pulled her to her feet. They started to run towards the station entrance.

Danny and Paul sat with their backs against the wall of a small underground room. A Dalek stood watchfully guarding them. There were two more at the other side of the room. Paul was still groggy. His head ached as he listened to Danny's whispered explanation of what he had seen.

'I was just coming round,' he said. 'David and Emilie were still unconscious. The Daleks took them off somewhere. Down there.' He pointed to the dark opening of a tunnel at one side of the room.

Before Paul could ask any questions, the Dalek moved nearer and commanded, 'You-will-remain-silent.' The boys did as they were told.

A moment later the fourth Dalek appeared from the tunnel. It reported to the others: 'Neutronic-charges-now-placed-in-key-positions-throughout-London-Underground-system. They-will-be-exploded-by-this-device.' The boys noticed the Dalek was holding a small electronic device which they presumed was a detonator.

The Dalek who appeared to be in

13

charge spoke next. 'We-will-now-start-
phase-two-of-the-operation.'

As one the Daleks answered, 'We-obey,'
the Dalek leader turned and moved across
to the boys. 'You-will-obey-our-orders.
Any-attempt-to-escape-and-you-will-be-
exterminated!'

David and Emilie had to fight their way
through the crowds to reach the police
barricade that surrounded the station
entrance. There was so much shouting and
running back and forth they could get no
one to listen to them. In desperation,
Emilie grabbed at a policeman's sleeve.
'Our friends are trapped down there,' she
shouted. It was like a magic password.
The policeman looked very serious and
told them to duck under the barrier and
follow him.

As they did, David whispered to his
sister, 'Don't mention the Daleks. They'll
never believe us.'

They were questioned briefly by a
worried-looking army officer. He called

together a small squad of men and with the children they all went into the station. David led the way down the now motionless escalator and on to the damaged platform. Firemen had already cleared a narrow path through the rubble of the fallen roof. They squeezed through and David pointed out the tunnel along which they had tried to escape. They picked their way along to the iron door. The officer tried to open it but it remained firmly closed. He gave an order and moments later firemen were cutting at the iron with burners.

Emilie hugged herself with excitement. 'It's going to be all right,' she said. 'They'll get Danny and Paul out of there.'

The door fell with an echoing crash. David and Emilie were the first through and the troops followed. They ran into the underground room. Emilie stared about her in horror and disbelief. The Daleks had gone. And so were Danny and Paul. The room was empty.

## Chapter Three

Colonel Trent, the officer in charge, ordered his men to search the tunnel that led off the underground room, then he turned to stare grimly at David and Emilie.

'If this has been some sort of hoax,' he said menacingly, 'you're going to be in serious trouble. We've got more than we can handle without brats like you playing practical jokes.'

Before the children could protest their innocence, the troops came back out of the tunnel. The sergeant reported, 'No way out down there, sir. The roof has collapsed. Tunnel totally blocked.'

The Colonel nodded. 'All right. Take the men back up to street level.' The soldiers moved off and Trent glared at the children. 'You know that you could be charged by the police for causing a public mischief? And the very least you deserve is a darned good hiding from your parents!' He turned angrily to stride away.

'Wait a minute,' cried Emilie. 'We were down here. The four of us. Honestly.'

'Don't make it worse by telling lies,' the Colonel said. 'There are only two entrances. The iron door which we had to burn through, or along that tunnel which is blocked by a fall. You couldn't possibly

16

have been in here!'

Something glinting in the corner of the room caught David's eye. He darted forward and picked it up. 'Look! Look at this,' he said triumphantly, holding it out for the Colonel to see. 'It's Danny's torch, the one we gave him for his birthday.'

The Colonel looked at it doubtfully. 'Doesn't prove anything,' he said finally. 'It might have been down here for years.'

Emilie said, 'Look at the handle. It's got Danny's name on it. I wanted to have it engraved but we couldn't afford it, so I scratched it on there with a nail file.'

Trent examined the torch. Scraped into the chromium plate in spidery letters was the name 'Danny'. For the first time the Colonel looked as if he believed them. 'You'd better tell me the whole story,' he said.

David began. He started at the point where they'd heard the loudspeaker voice telling them to leave the station. Then he described the explosion. Emilie took up the story where they had come through the iron door. 'Then we couldn't believe our eyes,' she said. 'Standing right in front of us were four Daleks.'

She didn't have a chance to go on. Colonel Trent jerked as though he'd had an electric shock. 'Daleks,' he said. 'You saw Daleks down here?' The children nodded. 'Then why didn't you tell me before?' he demanded. 'We didn't think you'd believe us,' David answered lamely. By now it was quite evident that the Colonel did believe them and was taking them very seriously indeed. He started to walk around the room, then suddenly dropped to his knees and started to examine the hard packed cinder floor. 'There are tracks here,' he muttered to himself. 'They certainly could have been made by Daleks.'

David's mouth was dry with tension. Automatically he reached for the roll of mints in his coat pocket. His hand touched something unfamiliar. He took it out. It was a thin metal plate, gold in colour and about the same shape and size as a postcard.

'What's that?' asked Colonel Trent.

'I don't know,' said David. 'I just found it in my pocket, but I've never seen it before.' He handed it to the Colonel who examined it carefully.

'Do you know what it is?' Emilie asked.

He nodded. 'Yes. I've seen one before. It's a Dalek message plate. It's obvious now why the Daleks let you two go. They presumed you'd find this plate and take it to someone in authority.' Colonel Trent looked grim. 'Unless I'm very much mistaken,' he said, 'this contains an ultimatum from the Daleks. It will have to be dealt with at top brass level. Come on.' He turned to move.

Emilie hesitated. 'But what about Danny and Paul?' she asked. 'They're down here somewhere. Aren't we going to search for them?'

'At the moment, the important thing is to find out what the Daleks are demanding. And I must tell you frankly, that unless we can get the authority to agree their terms, I don't think your friends have a chance in a million of getting out of this alive!'

Danny and Paul had been forced to march into the tunnel at gun point. Shortly after they had left the underground room, one of the Daleks had fired a charge at the roof, bringing down a huge section that

18

completely blocked the tunnel behind them. Then the Daleks had prodded them along what seemed like endless miles of tunnels. The leading Dalek gave the order for them to halt. Ahead of them was a narrow opening and through it Danny could see the feeble glow of moonlight. Danny sniffed. There was the smell of freshly dug earth and there was mud under his feet. The Daleks must have found some way to burrow up to the surface, Danny thought. A Dalek made a careful check on the outside and then they all moved forward through the hole and out into London's cool night air.

Paul and Danny stared around. For a moment they had no idea where they were, then a cloud slithered away from the moon and they saw they were near the edge of the lake in St. James's park. Behind them the Mall, silent at this early hour of the morning. Ahead of them across the moonlit waters of the lake were Birdcage Walk and the solid dark block of Wellington Barracks. The Daleks stared cautiously all around them until they were satisfied they were unobserved, then they prodded Danny and Paul forward again and the whole group moved down to the very edge of the lake. The boys watched with amazement as one of the Daleks glided forward into the water, going deeper and deeper until it sank from sight. Danny considered the chance of making a run for it, but before he could make up his mind the surface of the water swirled and the Dalek reappeared. It was holding two black rubber face masks. Attached to each was a tiny metal cylinder.

'You-will-place-these-over-your-faces,' the Dalek intoned. The boys did as they were told. The two Daleks behind them pressed

the sucker cups at the tips of their arms
firmly between the boys' shoulders. Paul
tried to struggle free but the sucker cup
held him in a grip of iron.

'Move!' commanded the leading Dalek, and
the boys were propelled forward into the
water. Their struggles were useless. The
water rose above their knees. Over their
waists. Its icy chill was no colder than the
terrible fear they felt as finally their heads
were forced beneath the surface. The water
swirled for an instant and then calmed,
erasing all trace of Danny and Paul.

## Chapter Four

Colonel Trent hustled Emilie and David into the back of a police car. It roared away from Green Park station with its siren blaring and its blue light flashing. Ignoring the red traffic lights and 'No Entry' signs, it made a screaming right turn into St. James's Street, giving heart attacks to the few late-night drivers coming in the opposite direction.

They rocketed into Marlborough Road and then left on to the Mall. David peered over the driver's shoulder. The speedometer needle was flickering around ninety miles an hour. Emilie was flung on to David's lap as they made another skidding right-hand turn that took them past Horse Guards Parade. Moments later they halted at a private doorway in the Ministry of Defence building. Colonel Trent looked quite ashen as he climbed from the car.

The police driver nodded to him casually. 'Sorry it took so long, sir. The car needs to go in for a service.'

Colonel Trent had gone straight into a conference room, leaving the children seated outside. They had watched the comings and goings of a good many high-ranking service officers. Now two more men were hurrying toward the conference room. One wore spectacles and a worried expression. The other had a fawn raincoat and was smoking a pipe. He reminded David of Mike Yarwood.

Emilie nudged her brother excitedly and whispered, 'That's Roy Jenkins, the Home Secretary. And that's the Prime Minister.'

David stared. 'That's not Mr Heath,' he said derisively.

'Of course it's not,' Emilie said impatiently. 'It's Mr Wilson's turn this month.' Emilie knew about politics.

Ten minutes later the conference room door opened and Colonel Trent beckoned to them. Inside all the officials were seated around a long table. The children were given chairs and the Prime Minister gave them a friendly smile.

'Well now,' he said, 'to be perfectly honest and frank, we need your help. Colonel Trent will tell you the whole story.'

Trent cleared his throat and began rather formally. 'On Friday night military radar picked up a UFO.' Emilie looked blank.

'Unidentified Flying Object,' David explained.

The Colonel nodded and continued. 'It was tracked for a while and seen to be approaching London. Then we lost it. Now, thanks to you, we know it was a Dalek space craft. This Dalek message plate you found,' – he placed the gold-coloured metal rectangle on the table – 'do you know how it works?' They shook their heads. The Colonel rubbed the tip of his index finger across the plate. Immediately a Dalek voice sounded through the room. 'These-orders-must-be-followed-exactly . . .' Trent lifted his finger and the voice stopped. 'Clever, isn't it?' he said. 'The finger acts rather like a stylus on a gramophone record.' He stroked his finger across it at another point and again the grating voice emerged. 'Unless-our-instructions-are-obeyed-large-sections-of-London's-population-will-be-exterminated . . .' He raised his finger. 'I won't bore you with the whole message. What it comes down to is this. The Dalek space craft has run into mechanical trouble and they need vital parts to get back into space. You heard what will happen if we don't supply the parts.'

Emilie looked puzzled. 'Couldn't you just drop a bomb on them?' she asked.

Trent shook his head. 'No. For one thing they are holding your cousins as hostages, and for another, we don't have the faintest idea where the Dalek ship is hidden.'

'But what can we do to help?' David asked.

The Prime Minister took over the briefing again. 'The Daleks insist that you two act as the intermediary. The go-betweens. Perhaps because they'll recognise you. Perhaps because they think we don't dare to take any offensive action if there are children involved. Whatever the reason, they'll make contact with no one but you.' All the men seated at the table stared at the children. The Prime Minister's voice sounded very serious. 'To be fair,' he said, 'I must warn you that the situation is highly dangerous. So dangerous I've ordered the complete evacuation of this part of London, Westminster, Victoria, St. James's. By dawn there'll not be a single person left.' Emilie and David looked at one another. The Prime Minister spoke again. 'Well, what do you say? Will you take the risk and help us?'

There was what seemed a long pause,

then Emilie said, 'Just tell us what we
have to do.'

As the water closed over his head, Danny
had been quite convinced that the Daleks
were trying to drown him. Then he found
that with the aid of the face mask he
could breathe. He could see nothing in the
murky water of the lake. His head cracked
against something solid. There was a
metallic sliding sound, then a gurgle and
the water level started to fall very quickly.
Danny saw he was in a white-walled
room. Some sort of air-lock he supposed.
Paul stood beside him dripping and shivering.
The four Daleks stood in a tight group.
One of them pressed a wall control and a

panel slid back. The boys were pushed
inside. What they saw made them forget
their wet clothes, their cold and their fear.
There was a great central instrument
console packed with dials and flashing
indicator lights. There were control panels
and computers and banks of glowing
screens. 'It's fantastic,' breathed Paul, 'but
where are we?'

Danny stared around in fascination.
'There's only one place we could be,' he
said. 'Inside a Dalek space ship.'

A Dalek moved past them and made an
adjustment to an instrument. Behind a
glass dial a digital counter started to
flicker over numbers. One hundred.

Ninety-nine. Ninety-eight.

The Dalek moved towards the boys. 'If-the-Earth-creatures-have-not-agreed-to-our-terms-by-the-time-this-registers-zero-you-and-half-of-London-will-be-exterminated.'

The digital counter clicked on. Eighty-six. Eighty-five. Eighty-four . . .

## Chapter Five

A thin mist hovered over the lake and a watery sun began to erase the night. A pair of mallard slipped from their nest on the island and glided serenely toward the centre of the lake. They veered off course sharply in sudden alarm, frightened by something moving under the water. A finger-slim antenna broke the surface and rose several inches. The tiny lens at its tip, like an evil eye, seemed to peer around the banks of the lake and then fixed its gaze on the bridge.

In the space ship beneath the water the Daleks clustered around the scanner screen that showed the periscope's view. Danny and Paul stared nervously at the glowing colour picture. A Dalek operated a control and the angle shifted slightly to show the paths leading toward the bridge. Nothing moved. The park was totally empty. The periscope returned to its view of the deserted bridge. 'No-sign-of-contact-with-Earth-creatures. Prime-detonator-for-first-neutron-explosion.' A Dalek moved a dial on the radio-controlled detonator.

Danny glanced at the digital counter that was ticking off the time to zero hour. Fifty changed to forty-nine then forty-eight. 'Come on. Come on,' Danny muttered urgently. The periscope scanned the area again. It was still deserted. Paul swallowed hard. He knew the Daleks were not bluffing. If no contact was made, the first explosion was designed to devastate the area of Oxford Circus. The counter clicked down to forty. Thirty-nine . . .

Colonel Trent and a small group of officials stood near the corner of the park at the Westminster end of Birdcage Walk. The Colonel looked at his watch and then at Emilie and David.

'You'd better get started,' he said softly. Emilie nodded nervously. 'You're quite clear what you have to do?' the Colonel asked.

It was David's turn to nod. He felt the grim tension of the men around him. 'Couldn't someone come with us?' he asked in a pleading voice.

The Colonel shook his head. 'The Daleks will only make contact with you two. They specified you were to be alone.'

Emilie gave David what she hoped was a reassuring smile. 'We'll be all right,' she said. 'Come on. Let's go.' She started forward determinedly, David at her side.

Trent watched them moving away. He muttered to no one in particular, 'If the Daleks harm those children in any way, I'll . . .' He left the threat unfinished.

The children moved quickly across the dew-soaked grass. David shivered slightly, partly from the cold dawn air, partly from the fear that was knotting his stomach.

Emilie pointed. 'We'll get on to that path. It leads down to the bridge.' They moved on, then David halted and dropped to one knee. 'What is it now?' Emilie demanded impatiently.

'Shoelace undone,' David answered.

'Then hurry up,' she said. 'There's not much time.'

Watching the children, Colonel Trent silently willed them forward. It was only when David stood up again he realised he'd been holding his breath. He looked at his watch again. 'They'll never get there in time,' he hissed.

In the Dalek ship the scanner screen still showed the empty bridge. Danny stared at it as though hypnotised. Paul nudged him and pointed to the counter. It flicked from ten down to single numbers. Nine. Eight.

The Dalek leader grated an order. 'Prepare-to-detonate.'

Danny tensed himself. If there was some way he could get that detonator. If he could damage it. Put it out of action. With no clear plan in mind, he leaped forward to snatch it from the Dalek's hold. The Dalek sensed the attack. It swung its powerful mechanical arm in a short arc and caught Danny a blow on the chest that sent him reeling to the floor. The Dalek leader glanced at the counter as it flickered down. Three. Two. One.

The order cracked out like a whiplash: 'Fire!'

Paul screamed the words: 'Wait! Look, look!' He jabbed his finger toward the scanner. The picture showed Emilie and David walking to the centre of the bridge. The Dalek eased its hold on the detonator. Danny forgot the ache in his bruised ribs and relief washed over him like a warm Mediterranean wave.

Emilie and David watched with amazement
as the four Daleks appeared from beneath
the surface of the lake. They glided up
the bank and on to the bridge. In
accordance with the Dalek's instructions,
the children had been equipped with tiny
transmitters. The microphones were
attached to their coats. Through these the
Dalek's demands were relayed to a receiver
in the conference room at the Ministry of
Defence. The Prime Minister, Colonel
Trent and the others listened grimly as
the Dalek voice crackled through a hum of
static to make its demands. When it was
finished, the officials held a brief
discussion and quickly agreed there was no
alternative but to accept the Dalek terms.

Within an hour two heavy tractors had been driven to the edge of the lake. Frogmen had fastened cables to the Dalek ship. The engines revved. Tyres skidded, then bit into the ground. Inch by inch they moved forward. The sleek, gleaming hull of the space craft broke the surface and slowly edged up the bank on to dry land.

The four Daleks patrolled around their craft warily, ready to fire at the first hint of treachery. The frogmen and tractors were ordered out of the area. Apart from the children, only Colonel Trent was allowed to remain. He moved to the Dalek leader. His voice was very serious. 'The electronic equipment you need is being brought by helicopter from the space research station at Oxford. However, it will not be delivered to you until I am reassured that the two boys you are holding hostage are safe and well.'

The Dalek seemed to consider for a moment and then pointed to Emilie. 'The-child-will-be-permitted-to-enter-the-ship-and-speak-with-them-for-one-minute.' Emilie had no hesitation in entering the space craft. With the Daleks outside, she'd have a moment to be alone with her cousins.

Danny and Paul were standing at a small desk as she entered. She was delighted to see them and started to gabble her news excitedly. The boys would be released the moment the work was completed, Emilie told them. Then the Daleks would take off and everything would be all right.

Danny interrupted her chatter. He looked grim as he handed her a Dalek message plate. 'It's vital you get this to somebody, Emilie. It lists the location of the bombs.'

Paul chipped in, 'We heard the Daleks

talking. The bombs are radio-controlled. As soon as they're safely in space they intend to detonate them. That was the plan right from the beginning. That's why they came here. If we don't stop them, London will be totally wiped out!'

Chapter Six

Street by street, house by house and finally room by room the evacuation of central London continued. Protesting residents were moved in their thousands by fleets of commandeered buses, trucks, taxis and cars. Police and troops formed a ring of steel around the danger zone setting up barricades on every road. Traffic was in chaos. To the fury of early morning commuters, no trains were allowed to cross Thames rail bridges into main line stations. Air traffic control re-routed all flights to ensure they did not overfly the area. Only the helicopter from the space research station was allowed into the zone. As he neared his destination, the pilot stared down in awe at the incredible sight of totally empty streets where nothing and nobody moved. It was as though London had died.

   With Emilie and David, Colonel Trent watched the helicopter touch down beside the low gleaming hull of the Dalek space craft. Emilie was desperate to pass on what Danny and Paul had discovered, but with Daleks standing so close to them she dared not speak.

When the Daleks were satisfied that everything they had demanded had been delivered, they ordered the helicopter to take off.

The Dalek leader crossed to the Colonel. 'Repairs-will-take-precisely-one-hour. You-will-now-leave-the-area. The-hostages-will-be-released-immediately-before-our-take-off.'

Trent nodded. He was in no position to argue. The trio moved away. The moment they were out of earshot Emilie blurted out her news.

'The Daleks are going to detonate the bombs the moment they're in space!' She handed the message plate to the Colonel. 'Danny found this. He said it gives the location of the bombs.'

In the minutes that followed, Colonel Trent and his aides mounted a desperate search operation. It was a race for life. With every second precious, racing police cars took bomb disposal experts to the locations described on the Dalek message plate. If they failed, London would cease to exist.

Trent paced the conference room in growing despair. It seemed he glanced at his watch every few seconds. Thirty vital minutes had sped by before the radio crackled to life.

'Search party three,' a voice reported flatly. 'We have located the device.'

The Colonel nodded and muttered to himself, 'One down, five to go.'

Almost immediately another report came in. 'Search party six. We've found it.'

A senior airforce officer hurried into the room. Tense with concern he led Trent aside, out of the hearing of Emilie and David.

'The Cabinet have reached a decision,' he announced. 'If all the bombs are not recovered and de-activated before the Daleks take off, we're sending in a squadron of jets. There's just a chance we can destroy their ship before they can operate the detonator.'

Softly, Trent asked, 'And the two boys they're holding hostage?'

The airforce officer shook his head. 'We can't help them.'

Two more units reported they had located the neutron devices, then the fifth bomb was found. With only one more to go, hopes began to rise. They still had ten minutes. Major Tarrant, the explosives expert, came into the room. He was carrying the five bombs that had already been located. He set them carefully on the table. Each of them was no larger than a matchbox. They looked as though they were solid squares of gleaming blue metal. There was no sign of a crack, a join or a weld.

Tarrant tried to keep the emotion out of his voice. 'They're made from a metal I don't know. They have a strong magnetic field and will attach themselves to any other metal. If they are neutronic devices, then I calculate that each of them has the explosive equivalent of half a million tons of TNT.' Tarrant hesitated.

Trent urged him on impatiently. 'Save the lecture. Just get them defused.'

Tarrant stared at him. 'I can't,' he said slowly. 'There is no way to get inside these things. Any attempt to pierce the casing will set them off.'

The deathly silence that fell over the room seemed to stretch into eternity and was only broken when an excited Captain entered carrying the sixth and final bomb.

'We've got it,' he said. 'Couldn't report it. Our radio was on the blink.' He fell silent as he saw the grim expressions of the others.

Trent checked the time. 'Five minutes,' he said. 'We don't even have time to get them out into open country.' He turned to the radio operator. 'Order the jets to attack,' he said. 'The Dalek ship must be destroyed.'

Before the order could be obeyed, David made a sudden dash toward the table. He scooped the six tiny bombs into his hands and darted toward the door, yelling for Emilie to follow him. Before any of the men could move to stop them, they were in the corridor and racing for the stairs.

Trent barked an order. 'Stop those children!'

Before the sentry could react they dodged past him down the stairs and out into the street. Still clutching the bombs, they ran toward the park and the Dalek space ship.

Trent covered his face with his hands. The radio operator asked quietly, 'You still want the jets to go in, sir?'

Trent hesitated, then nodded. He knew his order was a death sentence on the four children. The operator pressed a key on the radio and the instrument suddenly surged with a violent crackle of static. The radio man looked alarmed. 'Something is jamming our signals!'

'Use the telephone link,' snapped Trent.

The man scooped up the instrument. From the ear-piece came a loud, shrill whine. He rattled the receiver. 'The Daleks must have full power restored on their ship They're blocking all our communications systems.'

Trent dropped into a chair, his eyes closed, his head bowed. 'Then that's it,' he said softly. 'We've failed.'

David and Emilie ran panting toward the Dalek ship began to rise. Slowly at first, remained outside. It swung toward them, its gun ready to fire, then recognising them, the Dalek lowered the weapon.

'You promised you'd let our friends go!' Emilie gasped.

Without a word, the Dalek glided into the ship, then Danny and Paul were pushed out. They stood blinking in the bright sunlight. The door behind them clanged shut. The space craft seemed to vibrate with power.

'Let's get away from here,' Danny shouted.

David stood beside the hull for a moment longer and then ran to follow his friends. The anti-grav motors surged. The Dalek ship began to rise. Slowly, at first, and then with astonishing acceleration it zoomed upward. In under a minute it was passing through the stratosphere and into the edges of space.

Colonel Trent watched through powerful binoculars. He knew that now the Daleks were out of range of damage by blast, London had only seconds to live.

The Dalek leader watched the fast-receding Earth on its scanner. It turned and glided across to where another Dalek stood beside the mechanism that would trigger the bombs.

'Detonate-on-my-command,' it grated. 'Now-Fire.'

The Dalek operated the switch.

The explosion was seen from almost all over Europe. A great, blinding flash some

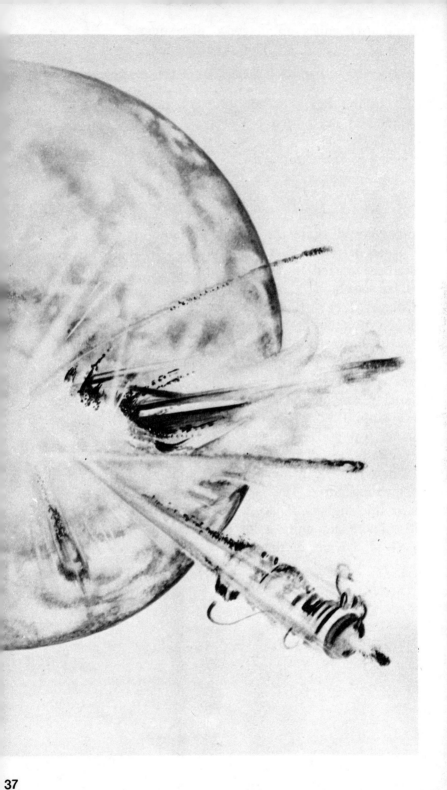

two hundred miles up in space like some mighty star exploding. The flare seemed brighter than the sun and lasted nearly thirty seconds, then it dimmed away to leave nothing but a million tiny fragments of what had once been a Dalek space ship and its crew. Debris that would drift aimlessly in space for ever.

The children stared down from a window in the Ministry of Defence. Cars and buses were starting to fill the streets again. People moved along the pavements and the dull roar of traffic that was London's heart-beat started to build up and pulse into life again.

Colonel Trent grinned at David. 'When did you think of it?' he asked.

David shrugged. 'When the explosives expert said the bombs were magnetic,' he answered. 'It just seemed like a good idea to stick them on the side of the Dalek space ship. I hope I did right.' The Colonel was still grinning as he led the four away.

'Where are we going?' asked Emilie.

'Downing Street first and then on to Buckingham Palace,' the Colonel said. 'There are quite a lot of important people who want to thank you.'

# THE DALEKS

## STORY OF A PHENOMENON

The Daleks provided the Doctor with something every hero needs – a worthy enemy. Just as Sherlock Holmes has the evil Professor Moriarty, the Doctor has the Daleks. The two are forever linked in an eternal struggle of good against evil. And that, of course, is part of the everlasting appeal of the Daleks. They are totally and utterly ruthless, interested only in conquest and destruction. Their metallic grating voices have one constant cry: 'Obey the Daleks!' And any opposition meets only one response: 'Exterminate!'

The Daleks are not only the most memorable monsters ever to appear on the 'Doctor Who' television programme, but they were also the first.

The first ever episode of 'Doctor Who' was broadcast on November 23rd, 1963. This adventure involved the Doctor, his human companions, and his granddaughter, Susan, in a journey into Earth's past and an encounter with some cave-men. The second adventure took them through time and space to the planet Skaro – and a meeting with the Daleks. A meeting that, for the Doctor, was to be the first of many. You can read about the Doctor's encounters with the Daleks later on, but first let's look at the impact the

Dr Who finds himself surrounded by Daleks outside the BBC Television Centre.

Daleks made on the viewing public.

To begin with, Terry Nation, who created the Daleks, nearly didn't write for the programme because of other work commitments. When he finally accepted the invitation he had no expectation that 'Doctor Who' would last for so long, and no idea that the Daleks were to become such an important ingredient in its success.

In his script he described the Daleks as *hideous, machine-like creatures. They are legless, moving on a round base. They have no human features. A lens on a flexible shaft acts as an eye, arms with mechanical grips for hands.*

It was the job of a BBC designer called Raymond Cusick to turn this description into reality. His first designs were too expensive to produce and he had to revise his plans to produce a simplified, money-saving version.

The final design was basically a simple pepper-pot shape inside which a very small actor could sit on a kind of office chair mounted on castors. The Dalek could be driven by the actor simply scooting it along the floor with his feet.

When they finished making the first Daleks, they were taken to the BBC car park to be tested. Verity Lambert, the producer of the programme, went along with the actors to where six Daleks were waiting, and the designer explained to the actors how to sit inside working the levers that operated the gun and eye-stalk.

'Suddenly the Daleks seemed to come alive,' Verity Lambert said later. 'The actors started to chase each other round the car park shouting, "I am a Dalek! I am a Dalek!" We all wanted to get inside and become Daleks ourselves.'

The Daleks had scored their first

success.

Soon children all over Britain were getting inside dustbins and cardboard boxes and waste paper baskets and shouting, 'I am a Dalek! Exterminate! Exterminate!'

Before very long, the country was firmly in the grip of Dalek mania! However, it took several years to realise the full impact of their success. At one time the BBC even gave some Daleks away to Dr Barnado's Children's Home – which suggests that no one realised that the Daleks would be coming back again and again.

The children at Dr Barnado's village in Essex were highly delighted with their gift. They had written to the BBC after the Daleks had been defeated and declared destroyed at the end of their first television serial, begging that the Daleks should not be killed off, and to their delight the BBC had presented them with two.

It was announced that two more Daleks remained in storage at the BBC, and the traditional BBC spokesman said, 'Who knows when they will appear again?'

Clearly, the BBC didn't yet realise what a success it had on its hands, despite the increasing numbers of letters coming into the BBC, demanding that the Daleks should return.

By now children in playgrounds all over the country were stomping round with outstretched arms bellowing, 'Exterminate!' and the press began to pick up and exploit the trend. An article appeared in the *Daily Mail* headlined 'DALEKS DEAD BUT WON'T LIE DOWN!' In it, Verity Lambert rashly said that there were no plans to bring back the Daleks in the

(1) Three young boys try out some Anti-Dalek toy weapons.
(2) A Dalek loose in Shepherds Bush, London.
(3) Jenny Linden and Roy Castle during the shooting of the film, *Dr Who and the Daleks*.

(1) Children from Dr Barnardo's enjoying the Dalek donated to them by the BBC.
(2) A Dalek meets his match with Frankenstein!
(3) A Dalek confuses passers-by when he lands on Westminster Bridge!

foreseeable future.

By 1964 pressure from public opinion was growing, and the BBC wisely decided that the Daleks had to come back. This created quite a problem for writer Terry Nation, who had to find a way of reviving the monsters he had first created, and then killed off. The building of more Daleks got under way.

By now the Daleks were appearing in more than just television. The well-known toy firm of Louis Marks produced the first battery-operated Dalek, and made record profits from the sale of that one toy alone. A version of this original toy Dalek is still in the shops today.

After this, Daleks of all shapes and sizes came on the market, from tiny ones at five pence each to four-foot-high ones that cost eight pounds. Woolworths were well to the fore in the Dalek boom, producing a wide variety of Dalek games including a Dalek version of the traditional 'bagatelle', and a number of Dalek jigsaws. Bagatelle wasn't the only game to be adapted. Even water pistols were being sold as 'fluid Dalek neutralisers'.

By 1965 the toy industry was Dalek mad, and the true Dalek fan could wake up in a bedroom decorated with Dalek wallpaper, go and have a wash with his Dalek soap, spar a few rounds with his inflatable Dalek punch-bag, put on his Dalek mini-badge and go out to buy his copy of a TV comic featuring a Dalek comic strip, or a Dalek book, DOCTOR WHO AND THE DALEKS – in those days there was only one!

In the shop he could also pick up a packet of sweet cigarettes, with Dalek cards in them of course, and a Dalek pencil. Back at home he could entertain his friends by playing a Dalek record, or give them a show on his *Doctor Who and the Daleks* Give-a-Show Projector.

The Daleks made an appearance at the *Daily Mail* Boys and Girls Exhibition in January 1965 and the queue to see them stretched for miles. Some children queued for three or four hours just to see the Daleks.

There were similar scenes whenever the BBC loaned out the Daleks to appear at some exhibition or charity fête. The Daleks had invaded the cinema as well, and by 1966 two Dalek films had been made, both starring Peter Cushing as the Doctor. The films had little to do with the TV series, though they followed the lines of the first two Dalek stories. The Doctor became a cuddly old eccentric scientist with a home-made time machine, and comedy roles were written in for Bernard Cribbins and Roy Castle.

The Daleks, however, retained all their old appeal, though they had developed one or two modifications in design and had a sinister habit of shooting out clouds of steam like animated electric kettles.

These two films still crop up on television occasionally, and are always showing somewhere or other as a matinée double bill during school holidays. Whatever their merits, they do give you a chance to see the Daleks in action during their periodic absences from television.

By 1966 the first wave of Dalek mania was subsiding a little, but this doesn't mean that the Daleks have been forgotten. There are still a number of Dalek toys and annuals on the market, and only recently the introduction of a 'talking' Dalek gave the toy market a whole new lease of life.

The Daleks have also appeared 'live' on stage, most recently in *Seven Keys to Doomsday* at the Adelphi Theatre in 1974

And of course the Daleks still continue their never-ending battle with the Doctor. The pattern is always the same. Whenever the Daleks fail to appear on 'Doctor Who' for a season or two, there builds up a steadily increasing demand for their return. And, of course, they always do.

*Destiny of the Daleks* is the eleventh Dalek story to date, and it seems highly unlikely that it will be the last. The hateful and unfeeling, but obviously fascinating, Daleks keep reappearing right through the sixteen-year history of 'Doctor Who'.

There are now no less than six 'Doctor Who' books featuring the Daleks, and more are planned for the future. So there will always be something to keep the dedicated Dalek fan going, even when the cry of 'Obey the Daleks or you will be exterminated!' isn't echoing from the television screen.

# INSIDE A DALEK

The major proportion of all research on Skaro is dedicated to the development and improvement of the Dalek. Incredible mechanical and electronic innovations have been made over the centuries all directed toward the aim, and the fulfilment of Davros's dream, of creating the perfect destructive machine. The Space Intelligence Service has released a report on its findings, but it must be recognised that many of the Daleks' inbuilt capabilities remain a mystery.

## A SCANNER
The 'eye' of the Dalek. It has telescopic magnification, Z and X ray capacity and infra-red night vision.

## B AUDIO-SCANNERS
Super-sensitive listening devices that are able to detect sound far beyond the spectrum of human hearing.

## C COMBAT COMPUTER
A memory cell containing every known war manoeuvre and strategy. Combat situations can be identified and reacted to in micro seconds.

## D PHOTO-SONIC CELLS
All images seen through the Dalek scanner and all sounds heard through the Audio Scans are stored here and are instantly retrievable.

## E ENVIRONMENT CHAMBER
The container in which the 'living' Dalek is housed.

## F GRAV DEFLECTORS
They allow the Dalek to remain in Skaro gravity conditions at all times.

## G PSYCH ANALYSERS
They give the Dalek the facility of what is virtually 'mind-reading' the thoughts of its enemies.

## H VOCAL SIMULATOR and TRANSLATOR UNIT
The Dalek has no voice. Its thought processes are converted into sound patterns and projected as the harsh grating speech that we hear via the simulator. The translator unit automatically converts the speech into the language of the listener.

## I ETHERIC TRANSMITTER/RECEIVER
Constantly operating sound and vision communications system directly linked to central command.

## J MULTI-RANGE VARIABLE POWER DESTRUCTOR
This small weapon is capable of penetrating armour plating at a range of more than three miles.

## K THE CONTROL ARM
A powerful vacuum, combined with hydraulic action allows the Dalek to hold and lift fantastic weights.

## L ELEMENT TO ENERGY CONVERTOR
This converts all the natural elements of the atmosphere into usable energy.

## M AUTO-NAVIGATORS
The unit is able to pinpoint precisely the exact geographic location of the Dalek anywhere in the Universe.

## N AUTO-REPAIR CIRCUITS
Linked to a computor, these circuits analyse faults and damage and repair the affected sections.

## O HOSTILITY SENSORS
These are able to detect aggressive attitudes in all life forms. The Dalek is aware of even a thought of hostility toward it.

## P CRYOGEN SURVIVAL UNIT
Under certain conditions the Dalek is able to induce a state of inanimation by 'deep-freezing' and thus preserving itself in perfect condition.

## Q AUTO-DESTRUCT
If capture cannot be avoided, or the computors assess the situation as hopeless, the auto-destruct circuits cut in. The Dalek remains dangerous even at this stage as it becomes a gigantic bomb.

## R MOTIVE UNIT
This allows the Dalek to travel at great speeds and to move with total mobility.

# DR WHO'S ADVENTURES WITH THE DALEKS

Since both the Doctor and the Daleks can travel in time, keeping track of their various encounters is by no means an easy business.

We can be fairly sure that *Genesis of the Daleks* is the first Dalek story, since in it we see the creation of the Daleks. Yet *Genesis* is one of the most recent Dalek stories to be shown, and in it the Doctor is in his fourth incarnation. And if *Genesis* is the first Dalek story, which is the last – or have we even seen it yet?

The Daleks seem to be destroyed at the end of almost every serial. Yet they always reappear with strength renewed, as full of malignant hate as ever. Perhaps the Daleks actually thrive on destruction, each setback only making them stronger.

Dalek fans have been busy for years, trying to sort out the chronology of the various Dalek adventures, and rationalising the many changes in Dalek social organisation and the frequent minor modifications in design.

Perhaps the best thing to do here is to take the adventures in the order in which we saw them on television. So here is a potted history of the Daleks to date – from the first Dalek adventure to the most recent . . .

We begin with *The Dead Planet*.

When the Doctor, still in his first incarnation, landed on the planet Skaro, he found a ruined world devastated by some long-ago atomic war. There were two groups of survivors: the metallic Daleks, at this stage confined to the corridors of their metal city, and the blond handsome Thals, living in the ruined wastelands of the planet.

Repelled by the emotionless cruelty of the Daleks, the Doctor took the side of the peace-loving Thals, and helped them in the struggle against their enemies. In an attack on the Dalek city, the Dalek power-source is blown-up. The Doctor leaves Skaro, confident the Dalek menace is over.

He has seldom been more wrong . . .

The Doctor didn't expect to meet the Daleks again – and he certainly didn't expect to find them on Earth. Yet that's exactly what happened in *The Dalek Invasion of Earth*.

In an attempt to get his human companions home, the Doctor lands the TARDIS in London. But not the twentieth-century London which they had left. This is a London of the future, a city almost destroyed in some terrible war.

A flying saucer passes overhead, a squat metallic shape emerges from the Thames and the Doctor realises with horror that the Daleks have invaded his favourite planet.

He discovers that the Daleks are mining in the heart of Bedfordshire, planning to remove the very core of the Earth, turn the whole planet into a kind of colossal space ship and take it back to their own star system. The Daleks are planning to

Dr Who, Ian and Susan in the BBC
Television Dr Who story, *The Survivors*.

steal the Earth itself!

With the help of brave human guerrillas, the Doctor defeats his enemies yet again, turning the colossal energies of their own weapons against them.

The Dalek invasion force on Earth is destroyed – but not before a final message is sent back to Skaro . . .

Back on Skaro. the Daleks plan revenge – a plan that is to lead to *The Chase*.

They develop a time/space machine of their own and begin a remorseless hunt for the Doctor.

The Doctor is forced to flee through time and space, aware that the Daleks are close behind him – and the gap is narrowing.

He is hunted through such unlikely places as the Empire State Building, the 'Marie Celeste' and the haunted house in a fairground, before deciding to stand his ground and fight on the planet Mechanus.

Here the Doctor and his companions are captured by the Mechanoids, a robot race who regard all organic life as specimens for scientific study.

The Daleks land and attack the Mechanoids in order to get their suckers on the Doctor. But the Mechanoids, with their deadly flame projectors, are more than a match for their attackers. Daleks and Mechanoids destroy each other in a savage battle and the Doctor and his companions escape. The Doctor is even able to use the Dalek Time Machine to project his human companions, Ian and Barbara, back to Earth – this time at the right date – well, give or take a year or two . . .

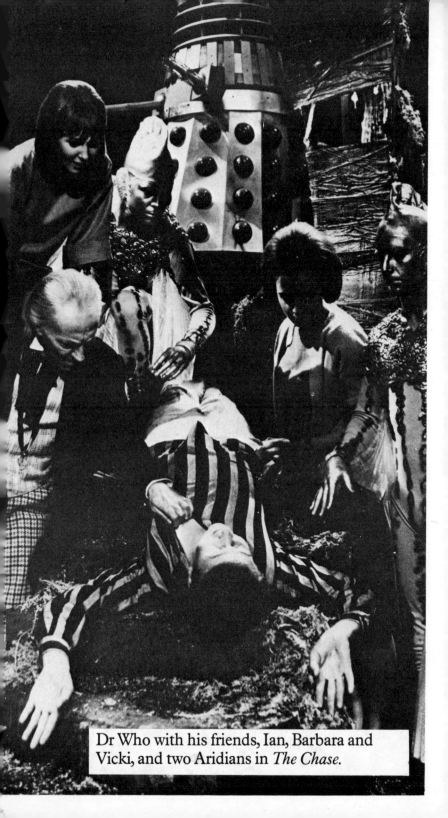

Dr Who with his friends, Ian, Barbara and Vicki, and two Aridians in *The Chase*.

The Daleks are able to identify space vehicles from
the smallest details. Can you outwit them? Match the
detailed parts shown along the bottom of the video
screen with the space craft.

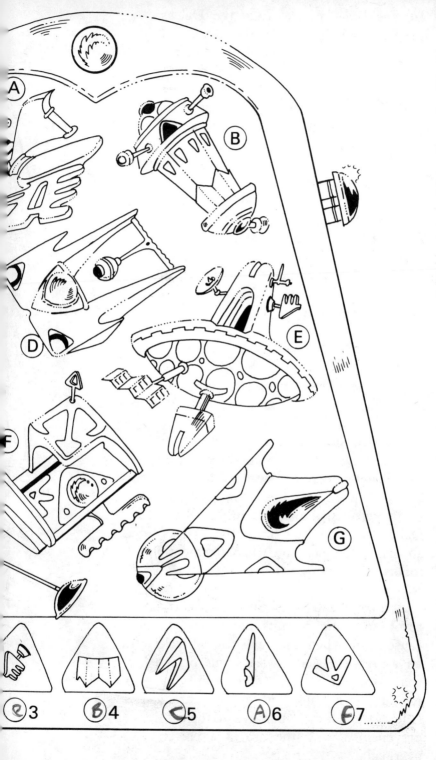

In *The Dalek Master Plan* the Daleks prepare their greatest and most evil scheme – the conquest of the Solar System, with their new secret weapon, the Time Destructor. The Guardian of the Solar Systems, Mavic Chen, has turned traitor, and is helping the Daleks.

The Doctor foils their plan by stealing the weapon's Tarranium Core – without it the Time Destructor is useless. Again, the Doctor and his companions are hunted through time and space by the Daleks. Although the Core is eventually re-captured, the Doctor foils the Daleks by prematurely activating the Time Destructor – which destroys its Dalek creators before burning itself out.

*The Power of the Daleks* is the first adventure of the Doctor's second incarnation. With his companions, Polly and Ben, he arrives on the planet Vulcan, now a colony of Earth.

A space ship containing three de-activated Daleks has been discovered in the planet's mercury swamps. Despite the Doctor's warnings, Lesterson, one of the Earth scientists, manages to bring the Daleks back to life. Since the Daleks appear to be no more than obedient robots, they are given the run of the colony.

Bragen, Head of Security, is plotting revolution, and recruits the Daleks to his cause. But when the revolution breaks out, an army of Daleks swarms out of the space ship, attacking loyalists and revolutionaries alike. Many lives are lost before the Doctor manages to defeat his old enemies with the use of a power-overload.

A menacing Dalek in *Dr Who and the Power of the Daleks.*

Victoria and Jamie are confronted by a Dalek in *The Evil of the Daleks*.

Dr Who has to neutralize 18 hidden Daleks to make this star city safe. Help him to find them. If you want more excitement set yourself a time limit. You can also colour this picture.

65

In *Evil of the Daleks* the Doctor's old enemies reappear not on twentieth but on nineteenth-century Earth. Aided by two renegade human scientists, they kidnap the Doctor, forcing him to aid them in their plans.

Jamie, one of the Doctor's companions, is subjected to a variety of dangerous experiments and the Doctor is forced to study his reactions in order to refine and isolate the 'human factor' – the quality of unpredictability and initiative which has caused the Daleks so many problems in the past. He is to transplant this quality into the Daleks, so producing creatures imbued with both human initiative and Dalek ruthlessness.

The experiment succeeds and the Doctor is taken back to Skaro where the Dalek Emperor tells him that he now has a new task – to spread the 'Dalek factor, Dalek ruthlessness and single-minded obedience throughout human history.'

Working at frantic speed, the Doctor manages to infect hundreds of Daleks with the 'human factor'. As he hopes, the newly-conditioned Daleks revolt against the others, and civil war spreads throughout Skaro as the Doctor and his companions make their escape.

The Doctor is to undergo a further change in his appearance, and to be exiled to Earth, before he encounters the Daleks again.

In *Day of the Daleks*, the Doctor investigates the appearance of mysterious 'ghosts' who seem to be attacking diplomat Sir Reginald Styles. The Doctor and his assistant, Jo Grant, are captured by a group of guerrillas. They have come from the twenty-second century to kill

The Chief Dalek in a scene from *The Day of the Daleks*.

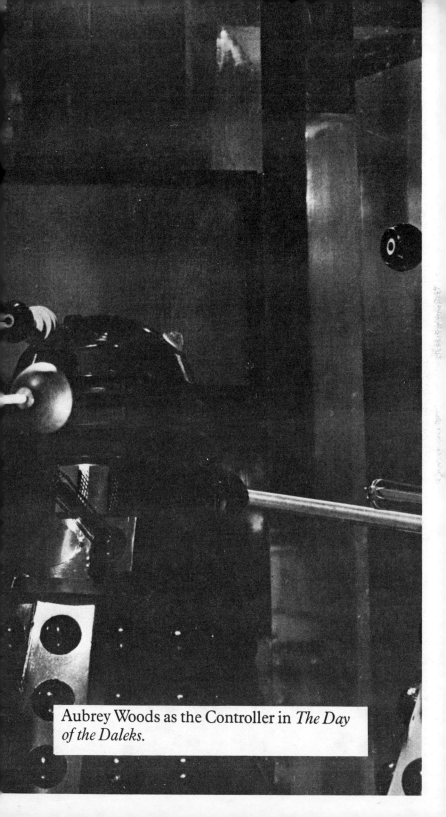

Aubrey Woods as the Controller in *The Day of the Daleks*.

Jon Pertwee as Dr Who is surrounded by Daleks and Ogrons in *The Day of the Daleks*.

Styles, whom they mistakenly believe to be responsible for the outbreak of a terrible war that changed human history. The guerrillas themselves are attacked by hideous ape-like monsters, who chase them back to the future. By the accidental use of a guerrilla time machine, the Doctor and Jo arrive in the future as well.

Here the Doctor finds a devastated world ruled by his old enemies, the Daleks. They have managed to alter the course of history and conquer the Earth. The Daleks invaded when Earth was weakened by a terrible world war, and the Doctor discovers that the guerrillas' planned assassination of Styles will cause this war, not prevent it as they hope. Only after a desperate struggle does the Doctor manage to prevent the assassination, defeat the Daleks, and return human history to its proper course.

In *Planet of the Daleks* the Dalek threat has spread to the distant planet of Spiridon. Dalek task-force has wrested the secret of invisibility from the natives. The Doctor joins forces with a Thal expedition, and mounts an attack on an underground citadel where an army of Daleks is waiting, frozen in suspended animation.

The Doctor and his friends finally manage to explode a bomb that triggers off an 'icecano' eruption, burying the Dalek army beneath thousands of tons of ice. The Daleks have suffered another setback, but as the Dalek Supreme boasts, they have only been delayed, not defeated: 'The Daleks are never defeated!'

The Daleks reappear in *Planet of the Daleks*.

Dr Who and Jo Grant deep in the Daleks' headquarters in *Planet of the Daleks*.

Lost in a Dalek maze, Dr Who has to reach the exit and safety. He can go under and over the passages, but not past a Dalek. There is a 60 second time limit!

In *Death to the Daleks* the mysterious and total failure of all power sources strands the TARDIS on the bleak and misty world of the Exxilons. The Doctor encounters a Marine Space Corps expedition in search of the vital mineral, Parrineum, the only cure for the space plague sweeping the galaxy. But the Daleks are after the mineral too, planning to use it to hold the human-colonised worlds to ransom. But the Daleks, too, have been affected by the power loss and for a time there is an uneasy alliance between the two expeditions.

The source of the power loss is the mysterious forbidden city of the Exxilons, a city which has grown so sophisticated and powerful that it has expelled its Exxilon creators.

The Doctor has to defeat the Daleks, help the Earth people to obtain the vital supplies of Parrineum, and destroy the power of the city, before he can leave the planet of the Exxilons and go on his way.

A burning Dalek in *Death to the Daleks*.

Dr Who has amazing powers of observation. He has
set you a test to help you develop yours. These two
pictures are identical except for ten small changes.
You have five minutes to pick them out. You can also
colour these pictures.

Dr Who, Peter Hamilton, Jill Tarrant, Don Galloway and Richard Railton accompanied by Daleks in *Death to the Daleks*.

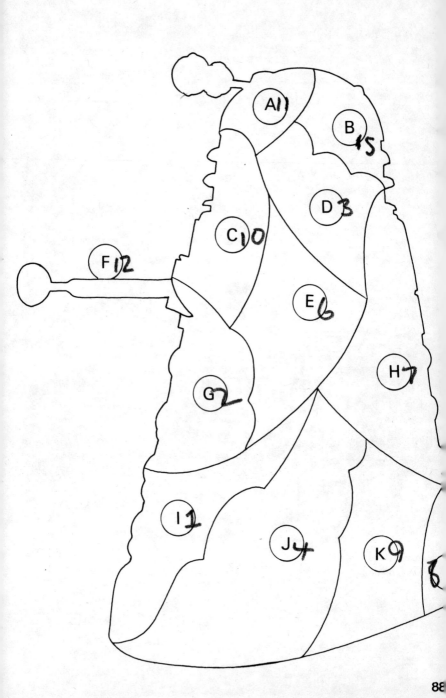

A1
B15
D3
C10
F12
E6
H7
G2
I1
J4
K9

88

Can you put the Dalek together? Don't worry, Dr Who has neutralized it.

Strangely enough, the next to last Dalek story is, in a sense, the earliest. *Genesis of the Daleks* takes the Doctor back to Skaro at a time when the Daleks are *about* to be created. He is despatched by the Time Lords on a mission to prevent that creation, or at least to modify its evil effect.

Skaro is in the throes of the long war between Thals and Kaleds. Davros, a brilliant, crippled Kaled scientist, has created the Daleks, the secret weapon that will enable his people to win the war. But Davros is too successful in his task. The Daleks turn upon their creator, and embark upon the course of ruthless aggression that is to spread throughout the galaxy. The Doctor barely escapes from Skaro alive, his mission uncompleted.

Yet strangely enough, the Doctor is not too unhappy. He knows that although the Daleks will bring centuries of chaos and destruction, out of their great evil some great good will finally come.

In *Destiny of the Daleks*, the latest Dalek adventure, the Doctor and his newly-regenerated Time Lady companion, Romana, land, not for the first time, on an apparently devastated planet.

They discover that the Daleks are already installed on the planet, carrying out some kind of excavation with the help of a work-force of slaves.

To his horror, the Doctor realises that the planet is Skaro, home-world of the Daleks, and the place where he first encountered them.

Also present on the planet is an expedition sent by the Movellans, who appear to be a race of handsome humanoids, opposed to the Daleks.

Davros, evil creator of the Daleks, in *Genesis of the Daleks.*

You can relax now. This is not another puzzle, but just
a picture for you to colour.

88

After many dangerous adventures, the Doctor discovers the terrible truth. The Movellans are a race of robots, as cruel and ruthless as the Daleks themselves. For hundreds of years the two robot races have been engaged in a ferocious war. But the battle fleets, and the battle computers that direct them, are exactly matched and the war has locked into a stalemate. Now the Daleks are excavating Skaro in order to find and revive Davros, the mad, crippled scientific genius, more machine than man, who first created them. They hope that the genius of Davros will give them the scientific superiority to break the deadlock with their Movellan enemies.

Davros is found and, thanks to his miraculously efficient life support system, is restored to malignant life. Accepted by the Daleks as their leader, his plan is to equip them with new weaponry that will make them totally invincible.

Thanks to the efforts of the Doctor and Romana, the Dalek plan is defeated and Davros is returned to Earth a prisoner.

Perhaps with the help of his knowledge, Earth scientists can find a way to defeat the Daleks for ever. But the Doctor knows in his heart that somehow the Daleks will always return . . .

Tom Baker as Dr Who with one of his deadliest enemies outside the BBC Television Centre.

# QUIZ ANSWERS

pages 58-59
1-D
2-G
3-E
4-B
5-C
6-A
7-F

pages 84-85
Did you spot these ten differences?

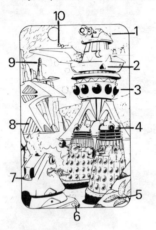

pages 88-89
A-11
B-5
C-10
D-3
E-6
F-12
G-2
H-7
I-1
J-4
K-9
L-8